MY VOICE IS MY SUPERPOWER

By Michelle Davey, MSW, LCSW-C
and Laiya Davey

Art by Remesh Ram

Guess what? I once was a little girl who didn't know how to use my voice to talk about what I was thinking or feeling. But now I'm using my superpower voice to tell you about the same power that's inside of YOU. I want you to use your superpower voice every day.

You can start right now by shouting,

"MY VOICE IS MY SUPERPOWER!"

MY NAME IS

_____
(Print your name.)

AND I AM A SUPERHERO!

This book is dedicated to all the SUPERHEROES!!
Your VOICE is your SUPERPOWER!

Acknowledgements

Our Wings Of Hope, LLC   Sweet Bites, LLC

Davey's Electric, LLC   Greta Be . . . Coaching

Pastor Dr. Mark & Queenie McCleary

Ck Family Services

Jonathan Noonan

Delroy Wilson

Scripture quotations marked CEV are taken from the Contemporary English Version. Copyright ©1995 by American Bible Society. For more information about CEV, visit www.bibles.com and www.cev.bible.

Scripture quotations marked ESV are taken from The Holy Bible, English Standard Version. ESV® Text Edition: 2016. Copyright © 2001 by Crossway Bibles, a publishing ministry of Good News Publishers.

Scripture quotations marked NIV are taken from the Holy Bible, New International Version®, NIV® Copyright ©1973, 1978, 1984, 2011 by Biblica, Inc.® Used by permission. All rights reserved worldwide.

Scripture quotations marked NKJV are taken from the New King James Version®. Copyright © 1982 by Thomas Nelson. Used by permission. All rights reserved.

Scripture quotations marked NLT are taken from Holy Bible, New Living Translation, copyright © 1996, 2004, 2015 by Tyndale House Foundation. Used by permission of Tyndale House Publishers, Inc., Carol Stream, Illinois 60188. All rights reserved

Illustrations by Remesh Ram
Book Design by Praise Saflor

Publisher's Cataloging-in-Publication data

Names: Davey, Michelle, author. | Davey, Laiya, author. | Ram, Remesh, illustrator.
Title: My voice is my superpower / Michelle Davey, MSW, LCSW-C and Laiya Davey; illustrated by Remesh Ram.
Description: Gwynn Oak, MD: Our Wings of Hope, LLC, 2021. | Summary: Little girls learn to use their voices to become empowered women of the future.
Identifiers: LCCN 2021920773 | ISBN: 978-1-7378259-0-6 (hardcover) |
978-1-7378259-1-3 (paperback) | 978-1-7378259-2-0 (ebook)
Subjects: LCSH Girls and women--Juvenile fiction. | Self-esteem--Juvenile fiction. | Self-reliance--Juvenile fiction. | Self-actualization (Psychology)--Juvenile fiction. | Christian life--Juvenile fiction. | BISAC JUVENILE FICTION / Superheroes | JUVENILE FICTION / Social Themes / Friendship | JUVENILE FICTION / Social Themes / Self-Esteem & Self-Reliance | JUVENILE FICTION / Social Themes / Bullying | JUVENILE FICTION / Religious / Christian / General
Classification: LCC PZ7.1.D3359 My 2021 | DDC [E]--dc23

Welcome!

Grab your FREE coloring pages by scanning the QR code or visiting our website at

www.myvoiceismysuperpower.com

I AM A VOICE in the morning when I open my eyes.

"Thank you, Father, for today's sunrise!"

From the rising of the sun to its setting, the name of the LORD is to be praised!

Psalm 113:3 ESV

I AM A VOICE as I sit at the breakfast table with my spoon in my hand, eating my favorite cereal and **singing**...

"THEY ARE MAGICALLY DELICIOUS!"

I AM A VOICE on my way to school,
saying my spelling word, **W-O-N-D-E-R.**
That means *something incredible!*
Yep, that's me!

8

I AM A VOICE as I remember my Father's words, **"Be strong and brave."**

I've commanded you to be strong and brave.
Don't ever be afraid or discouraged! I am the Lord your God,
and I wll be there to help you wherever you go.

Joshua 1:9 CEV

I AM A VOICE when I arrive at school and wave *"hi"* to the teachers who tell me that I can do all things.

I can do all things through Christ who strengthens me.
Philippians 4:13 NKJV

I AM A VOICE when I enter the classroom and settle at my desk. I am **ready** to do my best!

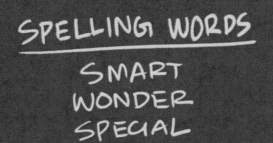

SPELLING WORDS

SMART
WONDER
SPECIAL

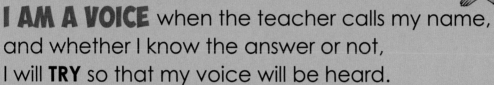

I AM A VOICE when the teacher calls my name,
and whether I know the answer or not,
I will **TRY** so that my voice will be heard.

13

I AM A VOICE in the hallway as the bully looks down on me, and with my eyes closed and knees shaking, I whisper "*no*" and run to the teachers to tell them the problem.

So be strong and courageous! Do not be afraid and do not panic before them. For the LORD your God will personally go ahead of you. He will neither fail you nor abandon you.

Deuteronomy 31:6 NLT

I AM A VOICE in the lunchroom, giggling with my friends as we swap and **share** our food so we each have the perfect lunch.

I AM A VOICE on the playground as I run up to the girl who sits alone and hasn't found her voice yet.
"Let's play," I say.

I AM A VOICE when the last school bell rings and I smile at my friends and remind them, **"It's been a good day."** YAY!

I AM A VOICE as I exit the school building and wave a **"thank you"** to the teachers who care so much about my education.

20

I AM A VOICE on my way home from school, talking about my day and praising myself for being brave in front of that bully.

Now I know that **fear does not control me!**

For God has not given us a spirit of fear,
but of power and of love and of a sound mind.
2 Timothy 1:7 NKJV

I AM A VOICE when I am back home, and when asked to do my chores, I answer, "**Yes, of course**," without any hassle.

I AM A VOICE after I finish my homework and look at my good job, and say, "**Well done**!"

I AM A VOICE at the dinner table as I pick through my vegetables and moan, **"Do I have to eat mine?"**

I AM A VOICE as I throw my card on the floor and yell, **"UNO!"** I love game night!

25

I AM A VOICE as I stand by the tub, doing my Floss dance, moving my hands and hips side to side, **waiting for the bubbles to rise.**

I AM A VOICE in the bathtub, playing with my dolls and teaching them that their PRIVATE and PRECIOUS parts are **OFF-LIMITS**. Just like that bully, if someone tries to touch me, I will run and tell EVERYONE, because my voice can SAVE LIVES!

I am fearfully and wonderfully made.

I AM A VOICE as I put on my pj's and tell myself, "I love you. You are **BEAUTIFUL**, you are **SMART**, you are **SPECIAL**... and you have a voice too!"

I AM A VOICE as I kneel and pray, "Now I lay me down to sleep, I pray the Lord my soul to keep. May the angels watch me through the night, and **keep me safe** till morning's light."

For he will order his angels to protect you wherever you go.
Psalm 91:11 NLT

I AM A VOICE as I snuggle up to Teddy and say,

"Night-night," looking to the Father for tomorrow's daylight.

You can go to bed without fear; you will lie down and sleep soundly.
Proverbs 3:24 NIV

I AM A VOICE in the morning when I open my eyes.

"Thank you, Father, for another sunrise!"

From the rising of the sun to its setting, the name of the LORD is to be praised!"

Psalm 113:3 ESV

Fun and thoughtful questions for easy conversations:

Superhero_____
(fill in your name)

 1 What do you like to talk about with your family?

 2 What do you like to talk about with your friends?

 3 What are some of the things you like to do with your voice?

 4 Why do you think your voice is important?

 5 How can you use your voice to help others?

ALWAYS REMEMBER THAT
YOUR VOICE IS YOUR SUPERPOWER

If you enjoyed this book, please leave a review.

bit.ly/MyVoice-Review

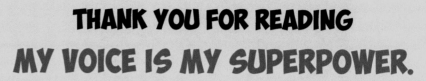

THANK YOU FOR READING
MY VOICE IS MY SUPERPOWER.

I am a licensed social worker and have been in practice for over fourteen years. During that time, I have had the honor of meeting many amazing women who have allowed me to walk with them on their healing journeys. Whether they were healing from trauma, from abuse, from low self-esteem, or from unhealthy relationships, there was an invisible, common thread woven through their stories: Their own VOICES could not be heard. No matter how many hours they sat in the chair in my office and talked and shared, even I could not hear their voices. Instead, I heard sadness, disappointment, depression, and even despair.

It is vitally important to begin nurturing a little girl's voice at a young age; if not, she might become a part of the next generation, sitting in my office chair, feeling stuck or broken. Together, we must work to help our daughters discover—or rediscover—and use their voices. This very thought, along with inspiration from my 8-year-old daughter Laiya, is what encouraged me to write this book.

I want to thank every parent, grandparent, aunt, uncle, guardian, social worker, teacher, bus driver, doctor, nurse, neighbor, pastor, and friend who is committed to not only hearing their own voices, but to also nurturing the voices of every child they encounter. And yes, your own voice may be the one someone remembers when going through a hard time. It could save their life!

Michelle Davey

ABOUT THE AUTHORS

Michelle Davey is a Licensed Clinical Social Worker who is passionate about empowering women. After experiencing her own traumatic events, she pursued a career as a mental health therapist. During her journey, Michelle chose to coach women who had lost their voices. She is inspired by the strength and resiliency of the women she has served and gains strength by being a part of their healing journey as they rediscover their voices.

Michelle is the founder of Our Wings of Hope (www.ourwingsofhope.com), an online platform that provides women with essential resources. She and her husband have three children and reside in Maryland. Michelle enjoys morning walks, roller skating, and reading books with her youngest daughter, Laiya, who is also the co-author of *My Voice Is My Superpower.*

Princess Laiya, who is the main character of *My Voice Is My Superpower,* is an energetic and bright 8-year-old. She is known as the "Voicer" because she is definitely one who voices her thoughts. She was an intricate and powerful voice in the process of birthing her first co-authored book with her mother. From the vague seed of an idea to the intricate details of each character, Princess Laiya divinely used her superpower – her voice. She even casually and wittingly injected her voice into the arena of web design. This smart, talented and inspiring young princess in the making will be a leading voice to be reckoned with for the lives of other young girls around the world – and when asked, she is up to the task.

Made in the USA
Middletown, DE
19 April 2023